Gifts

Phyllis Limbacher Tildes

TALEWINDS

An Imprint of Charlesbridge Publishing

In loving memory of
Carol and Carl Tildes

With special thanks to Chloe Zeldner
and my editor, Juliana McIntyre

A TALEWINDS Book
Published by Charlesbridge Publishing
85 Main Street, Watertown, MA 02472
(617) 926-0329
www.charlesbridge.com

Library of Congress Cataloging-in-Publication Data
Tildes, Phyllis Limbacher.
   Gifts/by Phyllis Limbacher Tildes.
          p.   cm.
   Summary: Presents the rhyming story of a young girl's
encounters with the gifts that nature has to offer.
   ISBN 0-88106-966-3 (reinforced for library use)
   ISBN 0-88106-965-5 (softcover)
[1. Gifts—Fiction. 2. Nature—Fiction. 3. Stories in rhyme.] I. Title.
PZ8.3.T454Gi 1997
[E]—dc20   96-27913

Printed in the United States of America
(hc) 10 9 8 7 6 5 4 3 2
(sc) 10 9 8 7 6 5 4 3 2 1

The illustrations in this book were done in colored pencil and
watercolor on Canson pastel paper.
The display type and text type were set in Sanvito by Diane M. Earley.
Color separations were made by Pure Imaging, Watertown, Massachusetts.
Printed and bound by Worzalla Publishing Company, Stevens Point, Wisconsin
This book was printed on recycled paper.
Production supervision by Brian G. Walker
Designed by Phyllis L. Tildes

A feather falls from way up high,
A soft gray curl against the blue.
It floats and dances in the sky,

Then lands so gently near my shoe.

I lift it to my sun-warmed cheek.
Its downy softness tickles me.

I picture wings, a tail, a beak,
And wonder what the bird could be

That gives its feathers freely.

Light flakes are floating in the breeze,
But it's too warm for it to snow.

The blushing dots held in my hand
Are petals of a flower so bright,

I jump and fall upon my knees,
And catch a few, so now I know

They sparkle everywhere they land.
Where are the blossoms, pink and white,

That give their petals freely?

A leaf blows past me in the wind
And rolls upon the mossy ground.
I chase it like a playful friend
And watch it turn and spin around.

It spirals upward, swirling high
And sails upon the airy sea.
I leap to snatch it from the sky
And wonder where the tree could be

That gives its leaves so freely.

Not far beyond I see the hill
On which there stands a gnarled old tree
That months ago in autumn's chill
Had sweet and juicy fruit for me.

I picked it round and red and ripe
And bit into its shiny skin.
I giggled as I tried to wipe
The sticky trickle down my chin.

This tree gave apples freely.

The tree has changed, for now it's crowned
In buds and blooms around its head.
The swaying branches near the ground
Invite me to come climb instead.

So up the knotty trunk I go
Far above the grassy mound,
And from the branch I'm just below
I hear a little peeping sound.

Who gives its song so freely?